The Princess Mouse

Told by
Aaron Shepard

Illustrated by
Leonid Gore

Simon & Schuster
London

Once there was a farmer with two sons. One morning he said to them, "Boys, you're old enough now to marry. But in our family we have our own way to choose a bride."

The younger son listened respectfully, but the older one said, "You've told us, Father. We must each cut down a tree and see where it points."

"That's right," said the farmer. "Then walk that way till you find a sweetheart. That's how we've done it, and that's how we always will."

Now, the older son already knew whom he wanted to marry. He also knew how to cut a tree so it fell how he wanted. So his tree fell and pointed to the farm where his sweetheart lived.

The younger son, whose name was Mikko, didn't have a sweetheart, but he thought he'd try his luck in the town. Well, maybe he cut the tree wrong, or maybe it had thoughts of its own, but it fell pointing to the forest.

"Good job, Mikko!" his brother mocked. "What sweetheart will you find there? A wolf or a fox?"

"Never mind," said Mikko. "I'll find who I find."

The two young men went their ways. Mikko walked through the forest for hours without seeing a soul. But at last he came to a cottage deep in the woods.

"I knew I'd find a sweetheart!" said Mikko. But when he went inside, he saw no one.

"All this way for nothing," he said sadly.

"Maybe not!" came a tiny voice.

Mikko looked around, but the only living thing in sight was a little mouse on a table. Standing on its hind legs, it gazed at him with large, bright eyes.

"Did you say something?" he asked it.

"Of course I did! Now, why don't you tell me your name and what you came for?"

Mikko had never talked with a mouse, but he felt it only polite to reply. "My name is Mikko, and I've come looking for a sweetheart."

The mouse squealed in delight. "Why, Mikko, I'll gladly be your sweetheart!"

"But you're only a mouse," said Mikko.

"That may be true," she said, "but I can still love you faithfully. Besides, even a mouse can be special! Come and feel my fur."

With one finger, Mikko stroked the mouse's back. "Why, it feels like velvet! Just like the gown of a princess!"

"That's right, Mikko." And as he petted her, she sang to him prettily.

> "Mikko's sweetheart will I be.
> What a fine young man is he!
> Gown of velvet I do wear,
> Like a princess fine and rare."

Mikko looked into those large, bright eyes and thought she really was quite nice, for a mouse. And since he'd found no one else anyway, he said, "All right, little mouse, you can be my sweetheart."

"Oh, Mikko!" she said happily. "I promise you won't be sorry."

Mikko wasn't so sure, but he just stroked her fur and smiled.

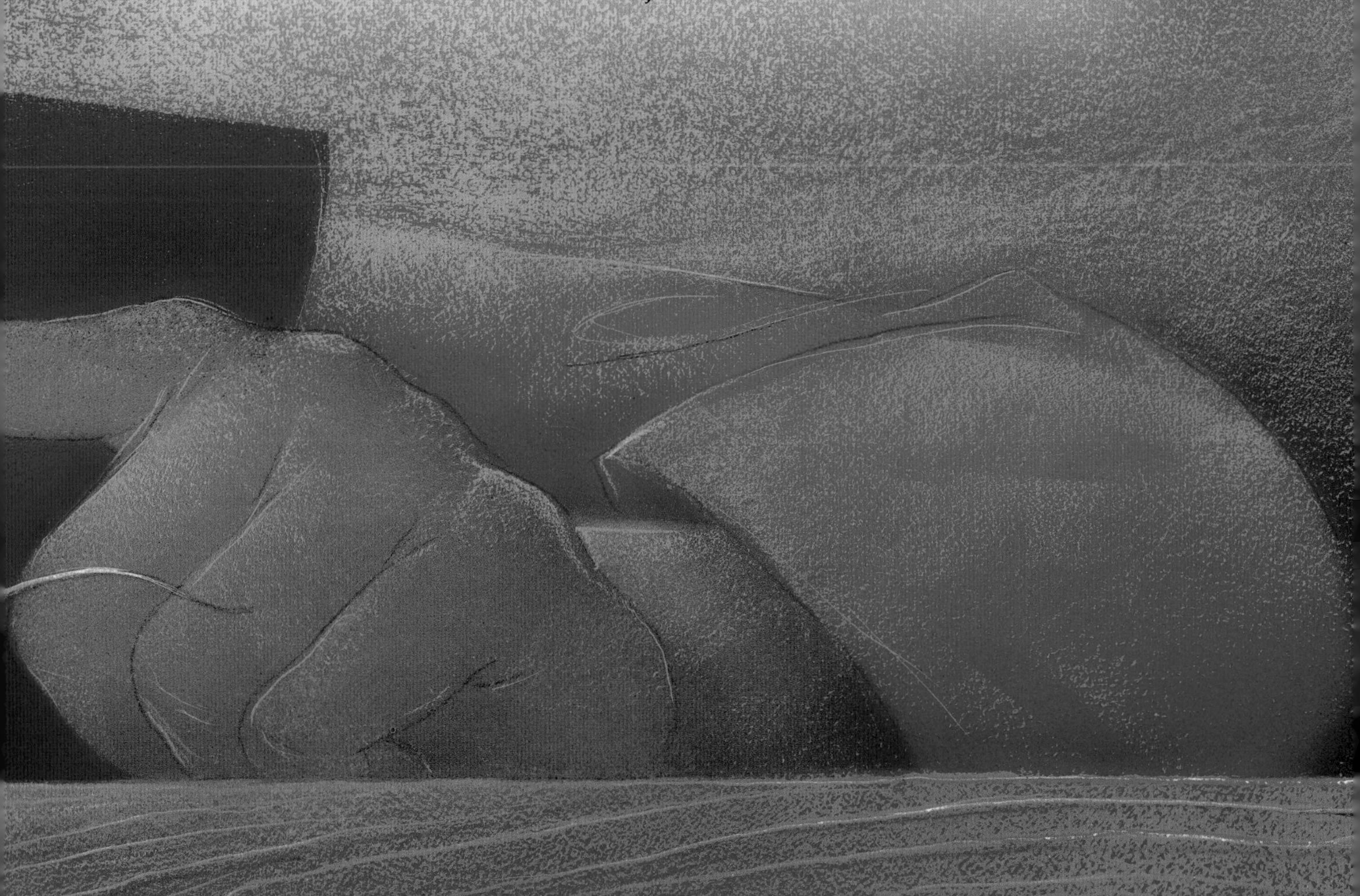

When Mikko got home, his brother was already there boasting to their father. "My sweetheart has rosy red cheeks and long golden hair."

"Sounds very nice," said the farmer. "And what about yours, Mikko?"

"Yes, Mikko," said his brother, laughing. "Did you find a sweetheart with a nice fur coat?"

Now, Mikko didn't want to admit his sweetheart was a mouse. So he said, "Mine wears a velvet gown, like a princess!"

His brother stopped laughing.

"Well!" said the farmer. "It sounds like Mikko's tree pointed a good way too! But now I must test both your sweethearts. Tomorrow you'll ask them to weave you some cloth, then you'll bring it home to me. That's how we've done it, and that's how we always will."

They started out early the next morning. When Mikko reached the cottage in the woods, there was the little mouse on the table. She jumped up and down and clapped her tiny paws.

"Oh, Mikko, I'm so glad you're here! Is this the day of our wedding?"

Mikko gently stroked her fur. "Not yet, little mouse," he said glumly.

"Why, Mikko, you look so sad! What's wrong?"

"My father wants you to weave some cloth. But how can you do that? You're only a mouse!"

"That may be true," she said, "but I'm also your sweetheart, and surely Mikko's sweetheart can weave! But you must be tired from your walk. Why don't you rest while I work?"

"All right," said Mikko, yawning. He lay down on a bed in the corner, and the little mouse sang him a pretty lullaby.

"Mikko's sweetheart will I be.
What a fine young man is he!
Cloth of linen I will weave.
I'll be done when he must leave."

When the little mouse was sure that Mikko was asleep, she picked up a sleigh bell on a cord and rang it. Out of mouseholes all around the room poured hundreds of mice. They all stood before her, gazing at her.

"Hurry!" she said. "Each of you, fetch a strand of the finest flax."

The mice rushed from the cottage but returned before long, each with a strand of flax. First they spun it into yarn on the spinning wheel. Then they took the yarn, strung it on the loom, and wove it into linen. Some mice worked the pedals, some rocked the beater, some sailed the shuttle back and forth.

At last they cut the cloth from the loom and tucked it in a nutshell.

"Now, off with you!" said the little mouse, and they all scampered back to their mouseholes. Then she called, "Mikko, wake up! It's time to go home! And here is something for your father."

Mikko sleepily took the nutshell. He didn't know why his father should want such a thing, but he said, "Thank you, little mouse."

When he got home, his brother was proudly presenting the cloth from his sweetheart. The farmer looked it over and said, "Strong and fairly even. Good enough for simple folks like us. And where is yours, Mikko?"

Mikko blushed and handed him the nutshell.

“Look at that!” said his brother. “Mikko asked for a cloth, and his sweetheart gave him a nut!”

But the farmer opened the nutshell and peered inside. Then he pinched at something and started to pull. Out came linen, fine beyond belief. It kept coming too, yard after yard after yard.

Mikko’s brother gaped with open mouth, and Mikko did too!

"There can be no better weaver than Mikko's sweetheart!" declared the farmer. "But both your sweethearts will do just fine. Tomorrow you'll bring them home for the wedding. That's how we've done it, and that's how we always will."

When Mikko arrived at the cottage the next morning, the little mouse again jumped up and down. "Oh, Mikko, is this the day of our wedding?"

"It is, little mouse." But he sounded more glum than ever.

"Why, Mikko, what's wrong?"

"How can I bring home a mouse to marry? My brother and father and all our friends and neighbours will laugh and think I'm a fool!"

"*They* might think so, indeed," she said softly. "But, Mikko, what do *you* think?"

Mikko looked at the little mouse, gazing at him so seriously with her large, bright eyes. He thought about how she loved him and cared for him.

"I think you're as sweet as any sweetheart could be. So let them laugh and think what they like. Today you'll be my bride."

"Oh, Mikko, you've made me the happiest mouse in the world!"

She rang a sleigh bell, and to Mikko's astonishment a little carriage raced into the room. It was made from a nutshell and pulled by four black rats. A mouse coachman sat in front, and a mouse footman behind.

"Mikko," said the little mouse, "aren't you going to help me down?"

Mikko lifted her from the table and set her in the carriage. The rats took off and the carriage sped from the cottage, so that Mikko had to rush to catch up.

While he hurried along behind her, the little mouse sang a pretty song.

"Mikko's sweetheart will I be.
What a fine young man is he!
In a carriage I will ride
When I go to be his bride."

At last they reached the farm and then the spot for the wedding, on the bank of a lovely, swift-flowing stream. The guests were already there enjoying themselves. But as Mikko came up, they all grew silent and stared at the little carriage.

Mikko's brother stood with his bride, gaping in disbelief. Mikko and the little mouse went up to him.

"That's the stupidest thing I ever saw," said his brother, and with one quick kick, sent the carriage, the rats, and the mice all into the stream. Before Mikko could do a thing, the current bore them away.

"What have you done!" cried Mikko. "You've killed my sweetheart!"

"Are you crazy?" said his brother. "That was only a mouse!"

"She may have been a mouse," said Mikko tearfully, "but she was also my sweetheart, and I really did love her!"

He was about to swing at his brother when his father called, "Mikko, look!"

All the guests were staring downstream and pointing and crying out in wonder. Mikko turned and to his amazement saw four black horses pulling a carriage out of the stream. A coachman sat in front and a footman behind, and inside was a soaked but lovely princess in a gown of pearly velvet.

The carriage rode up along the bank and stopped right before him. "Mikko," said the princess, "aren't you going to help me down?"

Mikko stared blankly for a moment, and then his eyes flew wide open. "Are you the little mouse?"

"I surely was," said the princess, laughing, "but no longer. A witch enchanted me, and the spell could be broken only by one brother who wanted to marry me and another who wanted to kill me. But, sweetheart, I need a change of clothes. I can't be wet at our wedding!"

And a grand wedding it was, with Mikko's bride the wonder of all. The farmer could hardly stop looking at her. Of course, Mikko's brother was a bit jealous, but his own bride was really quite nice, so he couldn't feel too bad.

The next day, the princess brought Mikko back to her cottage – but it was a cottage no longer! It was a castle with hundreds of servants, and there they made their home happily.

And if Mikko and the princess had any sons, you know just how they chose their brides.

The Song of the Princess Mouse

Words and music by Aaron Shepard

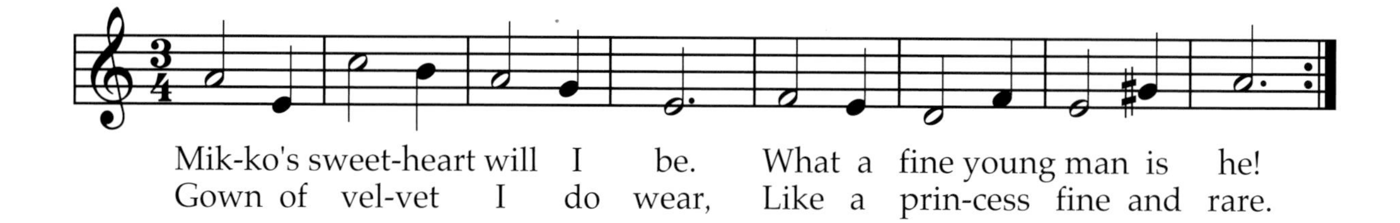

About the Story

My retelling is mostly based on the "The Forest Bride," in *Mighty Mikko: A Book of Finnish Fairy Tales and Folk Tales,* by Parker Fillmore (Harcourt Brace, New York, 1922). Fillmore's own retellings were based on folklore collections of Finnish scholar Eero Salmelainen, unfortunately still not available in English. I also consulted "The Mouse Bride," in *Tales from a Finnish Tupa,* by James Cloyd Bowman and Margery Bianco (Albert Whitman, Chicago, 1940).

For a reader's theatre script of this story, a recording of the tune from the princess mouse's song, and another test of the brothers' sweethearts, visit my home page at www.aaronshep.com

Aaron Shepard

Again, for Anne

– A. S.

For Michael E. and his parents

– L. G.

First published in Great Britain in 2003 by Simon & Schuster UK Ltd
Africa House, 64-78 Kingsway, London WC2B 6AH

Book design by Abelardo Martinez
The text for this book is set in Hiroshige. The illustrations are rendered in acrylic and pastel on paper.
A CIP catalogue record for this book is available from the British Library upon request

0-689-83697x

Manufactured in China

1 3 5 7 9 10 8 6 4 2